I Never Win!

I Never Win!

by JUDY DELTON
pictures by CATHY GILCHRIST

Carolrhoda Books · Minneapolis, Minnesota

For Joanne
—J.D.

For Jeremy
—C.G.

LIBRARY OF CONGRESS CATALOGING IN PUBLICATION DATA

Delton, Judy.
I never win!

(A Carolrhoda on my own book)
SUMMARY: Charles becomes increasingly frustrated
as he watches everyone else win prizes.

[1. Winning and losing—Fiction] I. Gilchrist, Cathy.
II. Title.

PZ7.D388Ian   [E]   80-27618
ISBN 0-87614-139-4

    1 2 3 4 5 6 7 8 9 10 86 85 84 83 82 81

I never ever win.

In the sack race

on the last day of school,

I came in second.

In Monopoly,
I always land on Boardwalk
when I don't own it.

On the first day of Little League,

I struck out.

I never win.

Last week I went
to Clara Perkins's birthday party.
Before we ate cake and ice cream,
and before she opened her presents,
we played games.
I hate to play games.
When we played Musical Chairs,
I was the only one without a chair.
When we played
Drop-the-Clothespin-in-the-Bottle,
I didn't get any in.
When we played
Pin-the-Tail-on-the-Donkey,
I pinned mine on the door.

Laurie got ten pins in the bottle
and won a Frisbee.
Tim pinned the tail where it should be
and won some colored pencils.
Robin Ames won Musical Chairs
and got a puzzle.
I like puzzles.
But I didn't even come close.

When the party was over,
I went home with no prize
and practiced my piano lesson.
I played the scales over and over
real fast because I was so mad.

On Monday Grandpa came for dinner.

After dinner we played checkers.

When we were through,

he sat back in his chair.

"Looks like you better practice up,

Charlie," he said.

"I beat you all four games."

Then he got up and lit his pipe

and said he would see me next week.

I'm not going to play checkers

ever again.

With anyone.

15

Wednesday we went to a pot-luck dinner.

Afterwards we played Bingo.

Mom won a lamp.

My brother won an alarm clock.

All I needed was B-9.

I waited and waited.
Then the man called, "G-51,"
and a lady in the back screamed,
"Bingo!"
She won a radio.

"I never win anything!"

I screamed at my mother.

"Why, Charlie, winning isn't everything.

Someone has to lose, you know."

"Why does it have to be me?"

I said as I carried her lamp to the car.

When we got home, I said,

"I'm going to practice my piano lesson."

"At this hour?" said my mother.

I played "The Flight of the Bumblebee"

faster than ever.

I played it over and over

until I didn't make one mistake.

Then I went to bed.

19

On Friday I went to the State Fair
with my friend Tim and his dad.
We rode the rides and ate cotton candy.
We were having a good time.

Then Tim said,

"Let's throw rings on the cat's tail

and win a panda bear."

He threw six rings

and won a little stuffed dog.

His dad threw six rings

and won a great big stuffed panda.

It was almost as big as we were.

Then I threw six rings

and the man said, "Sorry, Sonny."

I didn't win anything.

I never do.

Tim's dad let me carry the panda.

Everyone walking by thought I had won it.

But I hadn't.

24

When I got home,

I memorized "The Flight of the Bumblebee."

It took me three hours.

This morning the telephone rang.

It was Mrs. Teasley, my piano teacher.

She said she was having

some important people over that night.

She wanted me to play for them.

I said, "Me?"

She said, "Yes.

Will you be able to come?"

Mom said I would be there by seven.

#2467

27

I wore my best shirt
and pants and socks that matched.
I played "The Flight of the Bumblebee"
really fast.
I didn't even look at the notes.
When I finished, everyone clapped.
They said, "Please play it again."
Then they asked me
to play three other songs.
"Amazing!" someone said.
"A fine job," said someone else.
"I'm so proud of you, Charlie,"
Mrs. Teasley whispered.
"You are my very best student."

Then we ate sandwiches
and drank lemonade
and I felt like I was at
a birthday party
or the State Fair
or Little League
and won!

I guess not every prize

is one you can see.